The Unforgettable Un-adventure

and

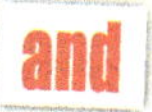

The Yeti Trap

Contents

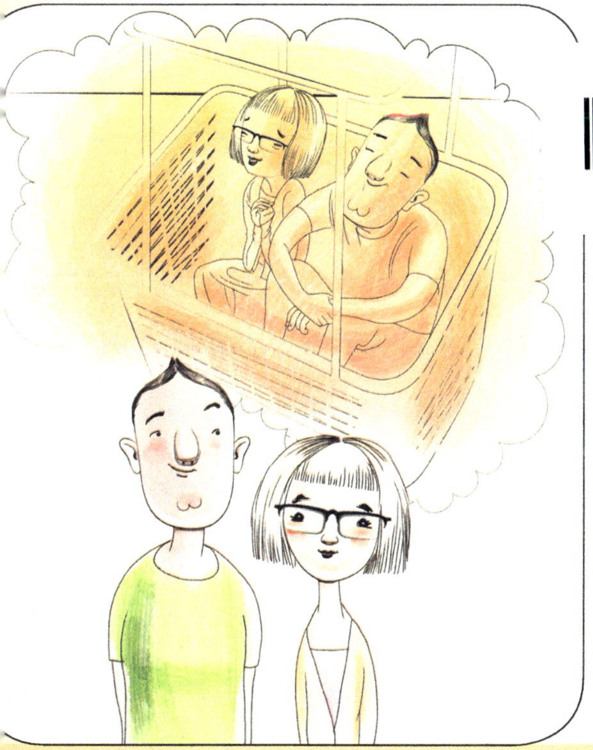

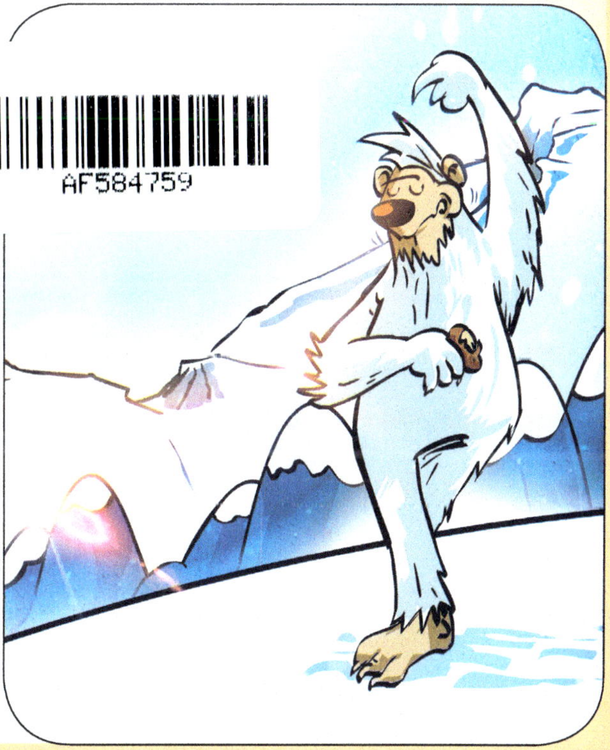

The Unforgettable Un-adventure

By Cameron Macintosh
Illustrated by Stuart Billington

Characters:

Narrator

Luke

Lily

Amy

Adam

Firefighter Nina

Firefighter Jake

Narrator

It's a fine February morning at the office of Adam and Amy's Un-adventure Tours for Timid Tourists. At 11 am, the door slides open and a pair of extremely unadventurous friends walks in from the street.

Adam

Good morning and welcome to Adam and Amy's Un-adventure Tours.

Amy

What can we do to un-excite you this lovely morning?

Luke

We're both in the mood for some extreme un-adventure.

Adam

Excellent! You've come to the right place.

Lily

We've tried off-road knitting, above-ground caving, even extreme power-snoozing. None of it was un-adventurous enough. We hope you can help.

Amy

I'm sure we can!

Luke

We were wondering if you could fit us in for some indoor windsurfing.

Adam

I'm sorry, but that activity is fully booked today.

Lily

That's a shame.

Amy

Perhaps we could interest you in a spot of bungee bouncing instead?

Luke

I'm not sure what that is.

Amy

It's the ultimate un-adventure. Harnessed to an overhead bungee cord, you'll bounce up and down on a trampoline. It's the closest you'll get to bungee jumping without the risk of any fear or excitement.

Lily

I'm sorry, trampolines give me motion sickness.

Adam

Well then, how about horizontal rock climbing?

Luke

I haven't heard of that.

Adam

With kneepads and protective gloves, you'll crawl at your own pace across a series of perfectly flat rocks.

Lily

That sounds fantastically un-adventurous!

Amy

Yes, it's a very popular activity.

Luke

Sorry, I've still got sore knees from a slowest-crawler competition last week.

Adam

How about some on-shore snorkelling then? In wetsuit and snorkel, you'll walk beside a pond full of goldfish, enjoying all the thrills of snorkelling without the bother of getting wet.

Luke

Sorry, I'm terrified of goldfish.

Amy

I've got it! You absolutely have to try cold-air ballooning. It comes with a money-back guarantee that it will bore you completely senseless!

Lily

It sounds a little bit too exciting for me.

Adam

Not at all! Comfortably seated in a cosy basket, you'll watch our cold-air pump inflate the balloon above you. It's one hundred per cent guaranteed not to ever leave the ground!

Luke

That sounds perfect! What do you think, Lily?

Lily

I've always wanted a balloon that didn't go up!

Amy

Great! Now I'll just have a look on the computer. Yes, we can book you in for 1 o'clock this afternoon.

Lily

That's perfect. Thank you.

Adam

We'll see you at Dozey Park in two hours, then. That's plenty of time to build up your un-excitement!

Narrator

Early that afternoon, Luke and Lily meet Adam and Amy at Dozey Park, where the cold-air balloon lies empty on the grass beside the basket.

Amy

Okay, if the two of you would like to climb into the basket, we'll fire up the cold-air pump.

Luke

In we go!

Lily

I'm having trouble containing my un-excitement!

Narrator

With Luke and Lily comfortably seated in the basket, Adam and Amy turn on the balloon's air pump.

Lily

Wow, it's filling up fast!

Luke

It's beautiful! All the benefits of flying without the stress of leaving the ground.

Adam

There you go – fully inflated. Relax and enjoy the … um … magnificent view.

Lily

What a view it is. The ground and the sky are both staying exactly where I like them to be.

Amy

We'll leave you in peace to make the most of it.

Luke

Thanks, guys, you've given us our most un-thrilling un-adventure yet. We couldn't be happier.

Adam

Our pleasure. We'll be back in an hour to let out the air.

Narrator

Adam and Amy wave goodbye and walk back to the office.

Lily

Ah, this is my idea of un-extreme adventure.

Luke

I can feel the un-excitement coursing through my veins!

COLD
HOT

Narrator

Luke stands up to have a better look at the view. He doesn't notice his head bumping the cold-air switch and flicking it suddenly into hot-air mode.

Lily

What's that noise? It's coming from above us.

Luke

I don't know. It's very loud. But now it's stopped.

Lily

Woah! Did you feel the basket shake just then?

Luke

I don't understand. There's no wind at all today.

Lily

Oh, no! Luke, look up!

Narrator

Lily and Luke look up and see that the pump is heating the air in the balloon.

Luke

We're floating upwards!

Lily

This was not part of the deal!

Luke *(shouting)*

Amy!

Lily *(shouting)*

Adam!

Narrator

From four streets away, Amy and Adam hear the panicked voices and run back to the park.

Adam

Oh no! That's not meant to happen!

Amy

Don't panic. We'll get you down … somehow.

Adam *(shouting to Luke and Lily)*

There's a hot-and-cold switch on the side of the air pump. See if you can flick it back up to "cold".

Luke

I've found it, but … it's stuck. It won't go back up!

Lily *(shouting)*

The switch isn't going up, but we certainly are!

Adam

They're 20 metres off the ground!
What shall we do?
How can we get them down?

Amy

I know – I've got a bungee cord in my backpack. We'll throw it up to them!

Adam

Great idea!

Narrator

Amy throws the coiled cord up to the balloon. Luke catches it and dangles it back down.

Amy

Got it! Now we need to tie it to something. Can you see anything?

Adam

There's not a single tree in this park. Not even a swing or a bin we can use.

Amy

We'll just have to hold onto it, until …

Adam

It stretches all the way and …

Amy

We lift up off the ground too!

Lily

Don't worry, I've got my phone. I'll call the fire brigade. They'll have a ladder long enough to get us down.

Luke

If they come soon!

Narrator

As the balloon climbs slowly higher, Lily calls the fire brigade. The bungee cord stretches further and further, until …

Adam

Uh, oh. It seems we have lift-off!

Amy

Hold on tight!

Luke

Don't panic, I can see a fire truck!

Amy

I hope they're quick! I can't hold on much longer.

Narrator

The fire truck speeds into the park and pulls up beneath the balloon. The firefighters, Jake and Nina, can barely believe their eyes when they see Adam and Amy dangling from the balloon, ten metres off the ground.

Firefighter Nina

I think we'd better send up a ladder!

Firefighter Jake *(shouting)*

Hold on tight up there!

Fire & Rescue

Narrator

Jake and Nina send the ladder up to Adam and Amy. They grab on and start to climb down.

Luke

Don't forget the two of us up here!

Adam

We'll tie the cord to the ladder so you can't go any higher.

Narrator

With the balloon anchored to the ladder, Adam and Amy climb down to the safety of the fire truck.

Firefighter Nina

We'll retract the ladder and wind the balloon all the way down with one of our hose reels.

Lily

That sounds like an excellent plan!

Narrator

Slowly, the hose reel winds up the bungee cord until the balloon lands close to the fire truck.

Firefighter Jake

Well, you all made it back to land. Is everyone okay?

Luke

I'm very sorry, but I have to say, I actually found this unexpected un-adventure a little bit …

Lily

… fun!

Luke

Yes!

Lily

I have to confess, I slightly enjoyed it too!

Adam

And me! My heart hasn't thumped like that for years.

Lily

I think we might be back for more tomorrow!

Amy

And I think Adam and I might add some more slightly less un-adventurous activities to our list.

Adam

We certainly will! Anyone for slightly warm-air ballooning tomorrow?

The Yeti Trap

By Cameron Macintosh

Illustrated by Scott Fraser

Characters:

Narrator

Hayley

Mum

Connor

Dad

Narrator

It's the middle of the chilly Greenland summer, when the sun never sets and many places are still covered in snow.

The Harvey family is huddled together in a tent on the first night of the top-secret "photograph-a-yeti" mission they've been sent on. While they eat their dinner, they flick through a file of extremely unusual photos.

Mum

As a zoologist, I think I'm qualified to say that the white furry animal in these photos is much more likely to be a polar bear than a non-existent creature like a yeti.

Connor

But, Mum, look again at this photo. Polar bears can't do handstands!

Mum

I'm sure it's just the camera angle giving that impression.

Dad

As a wildlife photographer, I have to agree with Mum. It's just an optical illusion, caused by a smudge on the lens.

Connor

But look at this one. It's doing a military salute!

Mum

It was probably just a bear, scratching its ear.

Hayley

I can't believe any of you think it was a yeti or a bear.

These photos are all fakes, made by silly tourists in costumes.

Connor

You're all wrong, wrong, wrong! And I'm going to prove it.

Mum

I think you'll have a hard time, Connor.

No one has ever produced any convincing evidence for the existence of yetis.

Connor

Just you wait and see.

I'm going to set a yeti trap. It will give you all the evidence anyone could ever need.

Narrator

After dinner, Connor asked Dad if he could set up his camera. Dad set it up on a tripod at a safe but visible distance from the tent. Before he returned to the tent, he set the camera's flash to run nonstop.

Connor

If the yeti likes being photographed so much, he'll find this camera irresistible!

Narrator

Back in the tent, the family watches the flashing camera through an unzipped tent flap.

An hour passes, then two.

The sky stays bright in the 24-hour Greenland sun.

Dad

It's five to ten, folks. I think it's time to slide into our sleeping bags.

Mum

Yes, we need our energy for another big day of searching for make-believe mammals.

Connor

You just wait until tomorrow. If we don't find a yeti during the day, I'll make sure we see one at night.

Narrator

The next day, the Harveys trek through the snowy hills. Mum observes interesting nests and footprints, and Dad takes stunning photos of the icy hills.

But no one sees any signs of yetis or acrobatic polar bears.

Hayley

Well, that was a brilliant waste of a day!

Connor

Maybe the yeti is just feeling a bit shy.

Hayley

Or maybe the local costume shop finally ran out of yeti suits.

Narrator

That evening, as the family eats dinner, Connor has an idea for some extra encouragement to lure the yeti to the camera. He quietly rolls a potato off his plate and tucks it into his pocket.

Connor

Well, now that dinner's finished, I'd better go and set up the yeti trap again. I'll help with the dishes when I get back.

Hayley

You're seriously going to do all of that again?

Connor

I sure am. I'll prove the yeti's real if it's the last thing I do.

Mum

Okay, but make sure you wear your snow jacket. It's very windy out there.

Connor

Yes, Mum. Okay.

Dad

And dig the tripod into the snow a little deeper, please. I don't want it blowing over with my camera on it.

Connor

Okay, okay!

Narrator

Connor sets up the tripod and flashing camera in the same place as the day before.

This time, he digs the tripod legs deep into the snow and places his secret weapon in front of it – a delicious, steaming baked potato.

Connor

I hope the yeti likes vegetables!

Narrator

Connor returns to the tent to find Mum, Dad and Hayley relaxing with their books and journals.

Connor

Okay everyone, the trap is set again. Back in observation positions!

Hayley

Sorry, I'd rather finish my book, boring as it is.

Connor

Mum, Dad?

Mum

Okay, Connor. Just for half an hour. I'm really tired from all the walking today.

Connor

Only half an hour?

Dad

Yes, we gave it a good go last night, Connor. We all need our rest.

Narrator

For the next 30 minutes, Mum, Dad and Connor watch the flashing camera. Dad's eyes are the first to become heavy, then Mum's. Soon, even Connor is struggling to stay awake. That is, until a series of thunderous booms shake the ground beneath the tent.

Dad

What's going on?

Mum

I think there's an earthquake!

Hayley

Or an elephant disco!

Connor

You're all wrong – look at the camera!

Narrator

The family gasps as they look out at the flashing camera and see a huge white, furry creature with a potato in its hand, looking straight into the lens.

Hayley

Wow, we finally got to see a polar bear.

Mum

Hayley, that's no bear.

Hayley

What is it then?

Mum

I've never seen a creature like it … but it seems to be posing for the camera!

Connor

Like a ballerina!

Dad

It can only be…

Connor

A yeti!

Mum

It's strangely beautiful.

Dad

It seems to think so, too. And he seems to like my camera a lot.

Mum

Yes, he's inspecting it very closely.

Dad

A bit too closely – he's just lifted it off the tripod!

Hayley

And now he's running off with it!

Narrator

The ground shakes again as the smiling yeti runs for the hills, proudly clutching Dad's camera.

Connor

Dad, I'm sorry. This is all my fault. I'll get it back, somehow.

Dad

Don't worry about it, Connor. It's much too dangerous to chase a wild animal like that.

Hayley

Don't despair. I think I have an idea that might just bring the camera right back to us.

Narrator

The next day, the family doesn't leave the campsite.

Under Hayley's instructions, they set up another one of Dad's cameras and all of his photographic reflectors and umbrellas around the tripod.

Hayley

If this doesn't lure that snap-happy yeti back with the other camera, nothing will!

Connor

But how will we make sure he leaves the camera behind when he comes back?

Hayley

Leave that problem with me!

Narrator

That evening, the family watch through the tent flap once again as they eat their dinner.

Just as Connor starts clearing the dishes, the earth begins to shake. It shakes harder and faster as the yeti sees the makeshift photographic studio and starts running towards it.

Dad

Look, it's putting my camera back on the tripod!

Connor

And now it's doing a handstand again!

Mum

If only we could record his antics. The zoological community back home won't believe a word of this!

Narrator

Hayley slips out of the back of the tent with something under her arm.

Suddenly, a loud horn sounds and the earth shakes again.

Connor

The yeti's running away!

Hayley

Yes, but thanks to me and my foghorn, look what he's left on the tripod!

Dad

My beautiful camera!

(looks at Hayley)

Foghorn? Why do you have a foghorn?

Hayley *(shrugs)*

In case we got lost? In case we needed to scare off the yeti?

Connor

Quick, let's have a look at the photos he's taken with it!

Narrator

They all gather around the camera, with eyes glued to the viewfinder.

Connor

Oh.

Hayley

Oh no.

Mum

Oh dear.

Dad

It's just one out-of-focus image after another.

Connor

And we have to pack up and go home in the morning.

Mum

So there's still no hard evidence of yetis but, mark my words, we'll be back to get it!

Connor

We sure will.

Hayley

Next time, I'm building a yeti wardrobe and dressing room.

Connor

And I'm bringing a spare camera!